This Walker book belongs to:

_____

_____

GOING HOME

MARGARET WILD · WAYNE HARRIS

WALKER BOOKS

AND SUBSIDIARIES

LONDON • BOSTON • SYDNEY • AUCKLAND

For Olivia and Jack. MW

For Mary Mellis. WH

This edition published in 2009
by Walker Books Australia Pty Ltd
Locked Bag 22, Newtown
NSW 2042 Australia
www.walkerbooks.com.au

First published in 1993 by Ashton Scholastic Pty Ltd

National Library of Australia
Cataloguing-in-Publication entry:

Wild, Margaret, 1948-

Going home / Margaret Wild;
illustrated by Wayne Harris.

Rev. ed.

ISBN: 978 1 921529 04 7 (pbk.)

For children.

Hospitals — Juvenile fiction. Homesickness — Juvenile fiction.
Imagination — Juvenile fiction. Jungle animals — Juvenile fiction.

Other Authors/Contributors: Harris, Wayne

A823.3

Typeset in Gararond
Printed and bound in China

10 9 8 7 6 5 4 3 2 1

Hugo is in a small hospital
right next to the zoo.
He's much better and
wants to go home.
"Soon," says the doctor.
But how soon is soon?

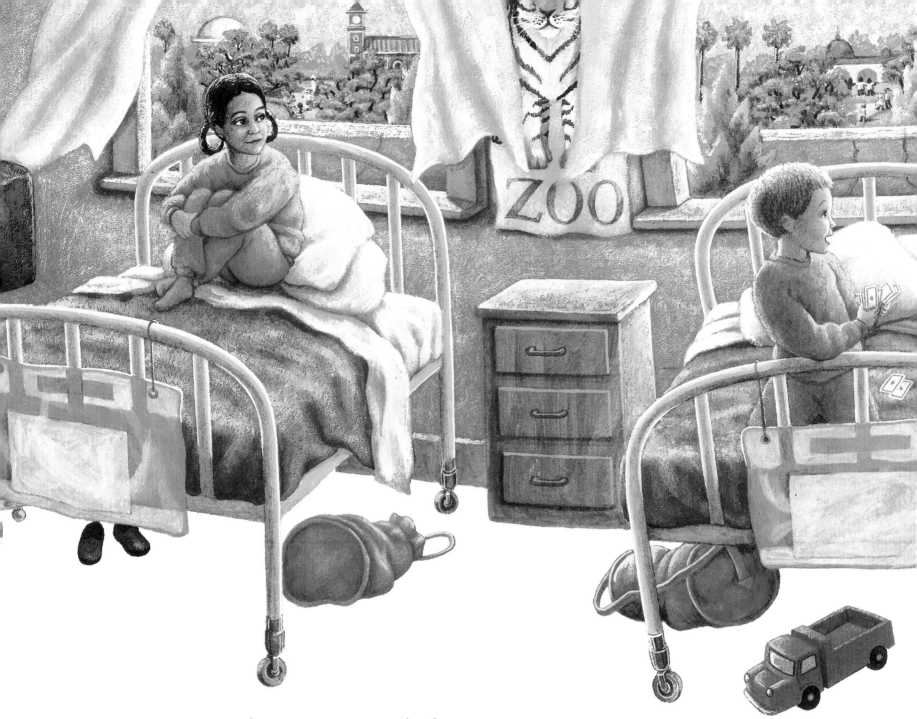

"Cheer up, it won't be long now," says Nurse Benny.

"Come and play cards," says Simon in the next bed.

"This is a really good show," says Nirmala who watches TV all the time.

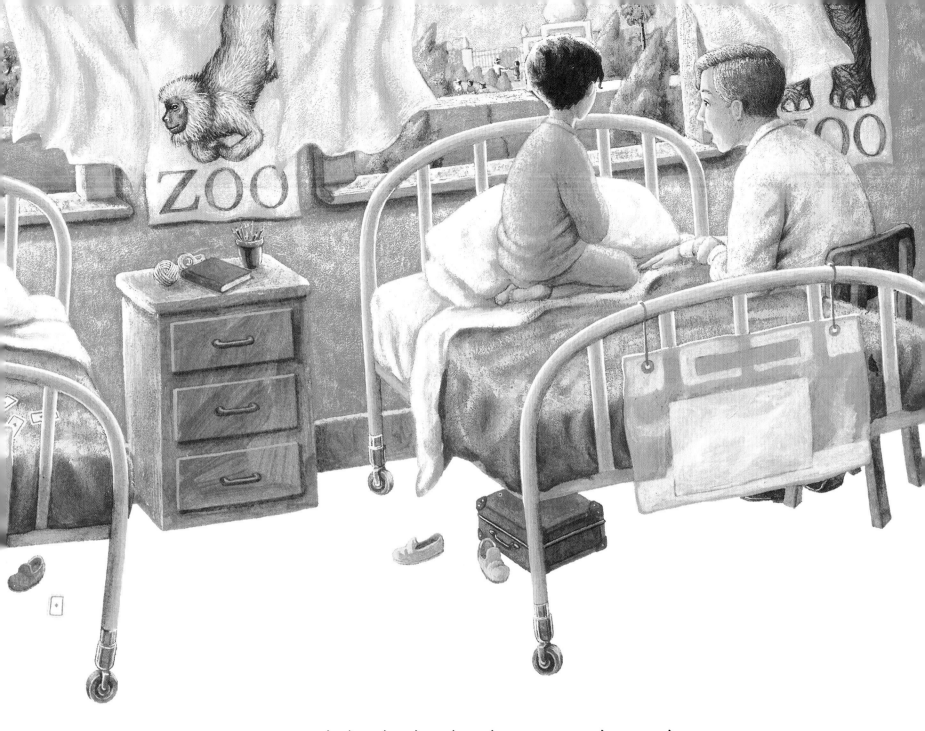

But Hugo shakes his head and stares out the window.
Right now Mum will be putting on the kettle and
his little sister, Cathy, will be playing dress-ups,
and his fat cat, Lucy, will be lazing in the sun.

So Hugo stares out the window, listening to the animal noises which float up from the zoo.

"What a racket," says Nurse Benny, but Hugo's eyes widen because an elephant is shrieking something special — a message just for him.

"Come, come home with me,"
shrieks the elephant, so Hugo
puts on his slippers — and goes.

He and the elephant amble through the
African grasslands, where lions play
rough-and-tumble games, and herds of
wildebeests migrate across the plains.

When his family comes to
visit, Mum asks as usual,
"So what have you been up to?"

"Quite a lot," says Hugo.
"I went to Africa."

"Lucky you," says Mum.

"It's not fair!" says Cathy.
"I only went to kindy."

So Hugo makes her a
little paper elephant
with flappy ears.

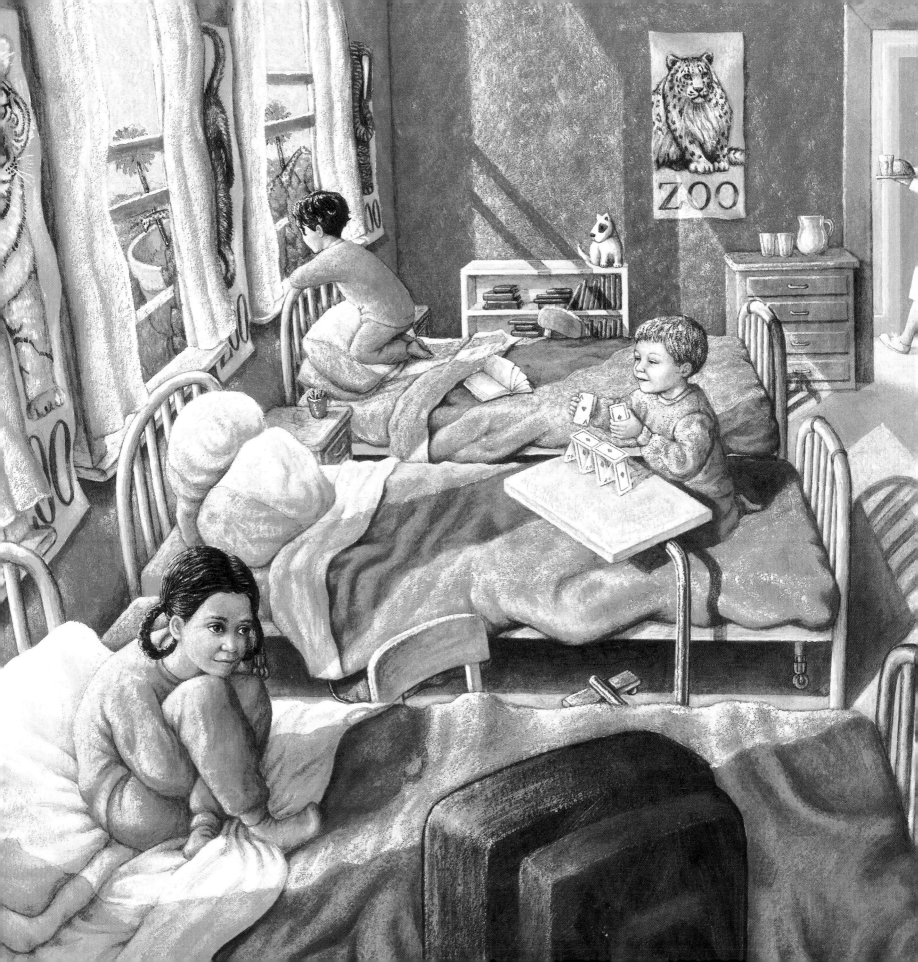

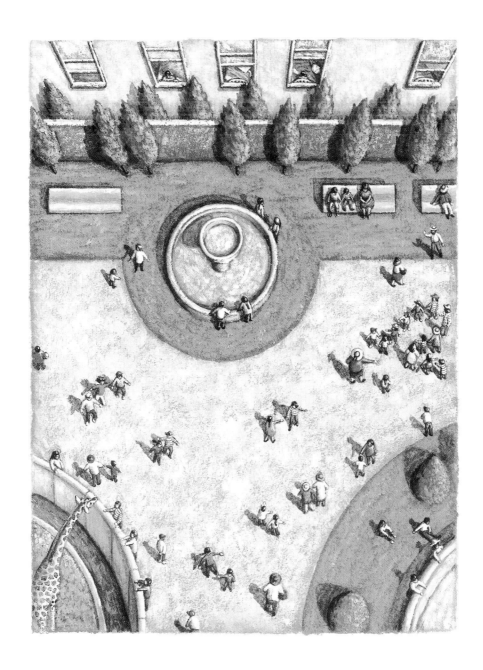

The next day while Simon is building a house
out of cards and Nirmala is still watching TV,
Hugo stares out the window and listens again.

The elephant is silent,
but the howler monkey is roaring,
"Come, come home with me,"
so Hugo puts on his slippers — and goes.

He and the howler monkey swing through the treetops of the Amazon jungle, where sloths sleep upside down, and the emerald tree boa hides in the leaves, and toucans gobble berries.

When his family comes to visit,
Mum says, "So where did you go today?"

"Quite far," says Hugo.
"I went to the Amazon jungle."

"Lucky, lucky you!" sighs Mum.

"It's not fair!" says Cathy.
"I only went to the corner shop."

So Hugo makes her a monkey puppet
which wiggles on her finger.

The next day, after Hugo has
played Snap with Simon and
watched a bit of TV with Nirmala,
he stares out the window.
And, very faintly, he can hear
the snow leopard growling,
"Come, come home with me,"
so Hugo puts on his slippers
— and goes.

He wraps his arms
around the snow
leopard's neck and
they hurtle through
snow and ice high
in the Himalayas,
where eagle-eyed
birds soar above
the slopes.

When his family comes to visit,
Mum says, "Been travelling again?"

"Yes," says Hugo,
"I went to the Himalayas."

Cathy stamps her foot.
"Not fair! I only went to the park."

So Hugo makes her a leopard mask,
and she growls and shows her claws.

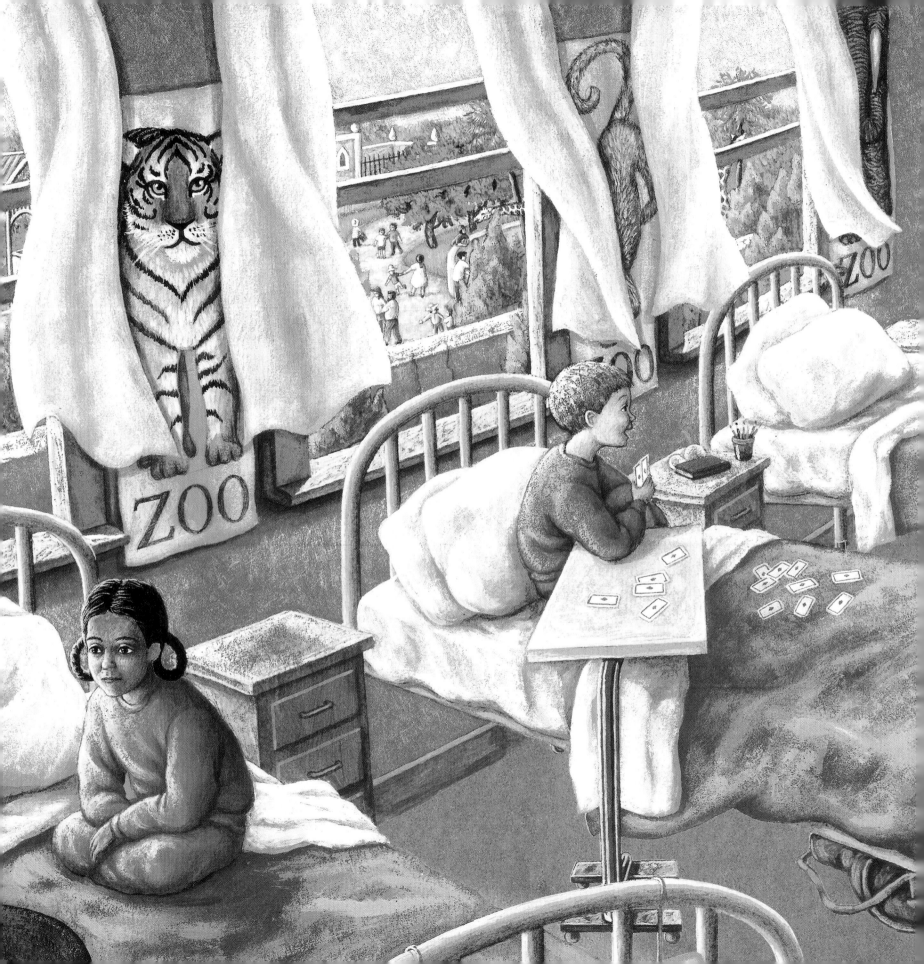

The next day when Hugo is just about to put on his slippers and leave for India, Nurse Benny says, "Surprise! Your mum and Cathy are here – you're going home."

"Come back and visit me," says Simon.

"I wish I was going home too," says Nirmala, and she watches TV harder than ever.

"I'll tell you both a secret," says Hugo,
and he whispers in their ears.

That night when Hugo is snuggled up
in his own bed in his own house at last ...

Nirmala and Simon put on their slippers ...

and run with the tiger
through the forests of India.

GOING HOME

Margaret Wild's text is deceptively simple. Its immediate charm lies in the beauty of the language, giving the tale such a poetic quality. But, like so many of Margaret's texts, the apparent ease of the storytelling belies the richness of meaning that lies within.

Even the title, *Going Home*, reveals the double sense of Hugo's impatience to be home with his mother and sister and the yearning of the captive animals for their natural habitats. That metaphor becomes more vivid still each time Hugo sets out on a new journey.

Like in all good fairytales, happenings come in threes: first Hugo's trip to the African grasslands with the lumbering elephant; then his rambunctious rollick in the jungles of the Amazon with the howler monkey, and finally, his liberating flight over the icecaps of the Himalayas with the snow leopard.

And, with each new adventure, comes the satisfying reunion with his mother and sister — Hugo making a symbolic gift for the young child — a gesture of inclusion and sharing, mirrored at the denouement by his shared secret with Nirmala and Simon.

Right from the first double-page spread, Wayne Harris gives us clues about what is to follow. His convincing children's hospital ward is decorated with posters of the very same animals that will transport Hugo on his journey. (For it is his larger journey that these fantastic journeys portray.) And we see as well, out of the window, the whole substance of the story reflected right from the outset — the stony barriers of the walls of the zoo and the colourful, busy activity of the visitors there who, unlike the animals, have freedom to come and go.

Wayne's thoughtful images invite us into Hugo's world. And we cannot help but feel for Nirmala and Simon who must secretly be longing for their own "escapes" as they distract themselves with television and creating houses out of cards. They each remind us, Nirmala, Simon and Hugo, of course, of the universal resilience, courage and resourcefulness of children.

So many clues in Wayne's illustrations reveal a complexity of meaning in the "space" left for him in Margaret's finely hewn text. Wayne creates such a feeling of movement with unusual angles that drama is added with every painterly composition.

What a joy that this delightful picture book has been reissued for new generations of young children and their parents to enjoy. *Going Home* is a superb example of a fine marriage between the author's tale and the illustrator's imagination.

ALBERT H ULLIN, OAM
Founder, first specialist children's
bookshop in Australia, established 1960

MARGARET WILD  has written more than seventy books and has been published around the world. Her numerous awards and distinctions include the Children's Book Council of Australia Picture Book of the Year Award for *Jenny Angel*, illustrated by Anne Spudvilas, *The Very Best of Friends*, illustrated by Julie Vivas, and *Fox*, illustrated by Ron Brooks. In 2008 she received the Nan Chauncy Award for an outstanding contribution to children's literature in Australia.

She and Wayne Harris have happily collaborated on many books.

If you've ever been in hospital, you'll know that the days and nights can seem very dull and long. And you're missing out on all sorts of interesting things happening at school and home with family and friends. So the most important question is, "When can I go home?"

It was serendipitous that Wayne Harris was asked to illustrate this story because as a child he'd spent a long time in hospital, and was able to draw on his own experiences and emotions to create illustrations that are both poignant and rich.

By using your imagination, you can escape an unhappy or boring situation and travel to exotic places without leaving your room. This is what Hugo does in the story, and Wayne's sumptuous pictures bring Hugo's imaginings to life.

Although I think the story is joyful and optimistic, it is also a little sad because although Hugo will be going home, we know that the animals at the zoo will not. My favourite illustration is the glorious painting of the snow leopard. (By the way, I love Hugo's golden pyjamas — I wish I had such a pair!)

I grew up in South Africa and came to Australia in the early 1970s. Like most people who have left their homeland, I sometimes felt homesick and nostalgic. By including African animals in the story, I was able to revisit familiar, much-loved landscapes.

A boy riding a snow leopard across the Himalayas.

A moment of freedom, exhilaration and enchantment.

An illustrator's dream.

I remember reading *Going Home* for the first time; I felt Margaret had peered into my own life.

At the age of seven, I was strapped and bandaged to a wooden frame in a children's hospital ward where all the patients had the same hip disease. Most were in traction for three months, the rare one for six; my sojourn lasted one and a half years.

It was an eternity. Days, weeks, months without being able to move, with nothing to hold onto but the edges of your imagination. Days of longing for your family, and feeling that "life" and fun were happening elsewhere. And days when friends in the ward were allowed to "go home" and you weren't.

Some forty-five years after my hospital stay I am still greatly moved by this story as "Nirmala watches TV harder than ever" when it's Hugo's time to go. And I invariably choke up at the end when Nirmala and Simon, with the gift of Hugo's secret, "run through the forests of India".

As an illustrator, my hospital experience gave me insight into Hugo's story — but at first the burden of the past produced dark illustrations, full of pain and abandonment. I was mistaking the story for my own. Margaret's words reveal the great resilience of children and I realised then that it was my job to empower the child reader. It was not about *me*; it was about *them*. So I stepped back and asked myself, "What am I trying to say to any child who might be going into hospital?"

Over the years I have come to count warmth, hope and kindness as cornerstones of good children's book illustration. They are the qualities that Margaret Wild understands completely, touched and shaped by her exquisite poetry.

WAYNE HARRIS has illustrated over thirty books, including *DragonQuest* by Allan Baillie which was shortlisted for Picture Book of the Year. Many of Wayne's illustrated books have received Notable Book status from the Children's Book Council of Australia.

Wayne is also a book designer, winning the APA Best Designed Picture Book of the Year Award for *A Bit of Company* by Margaret Wild, *Gordon's Got a Snookie* by Lisa Shanahan and *Two Bullies* by Junko Morimoto. He was shortlisted in the 1995 NSW Premier's Award for writing *Judy and the Volcano*, the same year *Going Home* was named an American Library Association Notable Children's Book.

WALKER CLASSICS

Walker Books is proud to be publishing these classic
Australian and New Zealand picture books.

Available from all good bookstores.

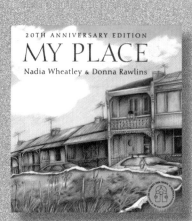

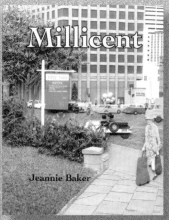